A PERFECT LOVE STORY RARELY EXISTS

MANAS KUMAR RAI

Dear reader,

As you begin to turn the pages of this love story, I want to take a moment to dedicate it to the ones who have made this book possible. This novel is a culmination of my thoughts, emotions, and experiences, and without the love and support of the following individuals, it would not exist.

I also want to dedicate this book to my parents, who have always been my biggest supporters. They have taught me the value of hard work, determination, and the importance of never giving up on my dreams. Their love, guidance, and encouragement have been a constant source of inspiration, and I am forever grateful to them.

To my friends, who have always been there for me through thick and thin. Your love and support have meant the world to me, and I am blessed to have you in my life. Your laughter, wisdom, and unwavering optimism have lifted me up and given me hope during the darkest of times. Thank you for always being there for me.

To my readers, who have been waiting for this book with bated breath. Your excitement and support have been overwhelming, and I cannot thank you enough for your love and encouragement. I hope that this love story will touch your hearts and bring a smile to your face, as it has mine.

Finally, I want to dedicate this book to all the people who have ever fallen in love. Love is a powerful and transformative emotion that can bring people together in ways that are beyond our understanding. Whether it's a love that lasts a lifetime, or a love that is fleeting, it leaves an indelible mark on our hearts. This love story is for all of you, for every love that has ever been and for every love that will be.

So, without further ado, I invite you to join me on this journey of love, heartbreak, and self-discovery. I hope that this book will bring you comfort, hope, and joy, and that it will serve as a reminder of the power of love to conquer all.

With love and gratitude,

Manas

Contents

Foreword

This novel is a tribute to the power of love, and to the resilience of the human spirit. It is a story that celebrates the beauty of a love that lasts a lifetime, and that reminds us of the importance of cherishing the ones we love.

In a world that often seems filled with darkness and sorrow, this story shines a light on the beauty of love, and on the power that love has to heal and to inspire. It is a story that will move you, and that will stay with you long after you have finished reading.

For those who have experienced the pain of losing a loved one, this story will offer comfort and hope. For those who have experienced the joy of a love that lasts, it will evoke memories and bring a smile to your face.

I am honored to share this story with you, and I hope that it will touch your heart as deeply . May it inspire you to hold the ones you love a little closer, and to cherish the memories of the ones who have passed. And may it remind us all of the importance of living each day to the fullest, for we never know when our time will come.

Preface

This is the story of a love so deep and so pure that it defined all odds and lasted a lifetime. It is a story of two people who found each other, against all odds, and who built a life together filled with love and happiness. But it is also a story of loss and heartache, of a love that was tested by time and fate, but that never wavered.

This is the story of Emily and Jack, two young lovers who met in the summer of their youth and who remained by each other's side through thick and thin, through good times and bad. It is a story of their love, of their commitment to each other, and of the bond that held them together through all of life's challenges.

This is a story that will touch your heart, make you smile, and bring tears to your eyes. It is a story of hope, of courage, and of the power of love. And it is a story that will remind us all of the importance of cherishing the ones we love, for as long as we are blessed to have them in our lives.

Acknowledgements

I would like to express my gratitude to all of the people who helped make this novel a reality. To my family, who always encouraged me and believed in me, even when I had doubts. To my friends, who supported me and provided a listening ear when I needed it.

I am especially grateful to my editor, who helped shape this story into the beautiful work of art it is today. Your guidance and expertise were invaluable, and I am so grateful for all of your hard work.

I would also like to thank the countless authors, poets, and storytellers who have inspired me over the years. Your words have touched my heart and have given me the courage to share my own story with the world.

Finally, I would like to thank the readers. Thank you for taking the time to read this novel, and for sharing your thoughts and feelings with me. Your feedback has meant the world to me, and I am so grateful for the opportunity to share my story with you.

Thank you all for your support, and for helping to make this novel a reality. I am truly blessed to have such wonderful people in my life.

The summer sun was setting over the small town of Willow Creek, casting long shadows across the quiet streets. Emily stood at the window of her bedroom, watching as the orange and pink hues of the sunset spread across the sky. She was lost in thought, her mind consumed by memories of the love she had shared with Jack, and the future that they had once dreamed of together.

They had met the summer , and from the moment she saw him, she knew that he was the one. Jack was unlike anyone she had ever met before. He was kind, and funny, and smart, and he made her heart sing. They had fallen in love that summer, and for the next few years, they were inseparable.

They had talked about getting married, about starting a family, about building a life together. They had made plans, and dreamed dreams, and thought that nothing could stand in their way.

But then, one day, Jack was diagnosed with a rare and aggressive form of cancer. The doctors told them that he had only months to live, and that there was nothing they could do to save him. Emily was devastated. She had lost her best friend, her soulmate, and the love of her life.

And so, she did what she had to do. She made the decision to put her own life on hold, and to be there for Jack, to help him through his final days. She stayed by his side, never leaving him, even when the pain became too much to bear.

And then, one day, Jack was gone. Emily was alone, left to pick up the pieces of her shattered heart and to try to make sense of the world without him. But even as she struggled to find her way, she never forgot the love they had shared, and the memories that they had made together.

Author's Bio

I'm passionate writer who has always been inspired by the power of love and the many forms it takes in our lives. With a background in creative writing and a love for storytelling.

My first love story book, "A Perfect Love Story rarely exists", is a testament to their belief in the transformative power of love. Through the journey of its characters, with its engaging plot, relatable characters, and heartwarming themes, "A Perfect Love Story rarely exists" is a must-read for them who believes that love is pure and a positive feeling.

I hope you will enjoy this journey.

Thank You

Author

What Is Love?

Love is a mind boggling and diverse feeling that can be challenging to characterize in only a couple of words. At its center, love is a profound sensation of friendship and association towards someone else, and is frequently described by sensations of warmth, delicacy, and defense. Love can likewise envelop a powerful urge for the joy and prosperity of the darling, and can propel people to act magnanimously and make penances for their friends and family.

Be that as it may, love can take a wide range of structures and can be knowledgeable about different ways. For instance, there is heartfelt love, which is portrayed by extreme sensations of energy and want, and is frequently connected with actual fascination and physical allure. There is likewise familial love, which is the profound fondness that relatives have for each other, and is frequently portrayed by sensations of solace, security, and commonality. Dispassionate love, then again, is the sort of adoration that exists among companions, and is described by sensations of trust, backing, and friendship.

Love can likewise be portrayed regarding its various aspects or viewpoints. For instance, there is the personal component of affection, which alludes to the sentiments and feelings that are related with adoration. There is likewise the mental aspect, which includes the contemplations and convictions that individuals have about their friends and family, and can incorporate things like deference, regard, and a feeling of shared values. At last, there is the conduct aspect of adoration, which alludes to the activities and ways of behaving that individuals take part in to communicate their affection, like thoughtful gestures, backing, and love.

At last, the importance and meaning of adoration can shift extraordinarily from one individual to another, and can be formed by a great many factors like social and strict convictions, individual encounters, and individual viewpoints. Certain individuals might characterize love as an extreme and energetic inclination that is all-consuming, while others might see it as a more quelled and consistent inclination that develops and develops over the long run.

No matter what its particular structure or definition, love is a general human encounter that has the ability to deeply impact our lives in significant ways. It can give us joy, solace, and satisfaction, yet it can likewise prompt awfulness, disillusionment, and agony. Yet, regardless of its difficulties, love stays a focal part of the human experience, and is many times seen as a wellspring of significance, reason, and satisfaction.

All in all, adoration is a perplexing and complex feeling that challenges simple definition. It envelops a large number of sentiments, contemplations, and ways of behaving, and can take a wide range of structures. Whether experienced as an energetic sentiment, a profound and standing fellowship, or a solid and rugged connection between relatives, love is a key piece of being human, and has the ability to give us pleasure, satisfaction, and significance in our lives.

1
Character Introduction...

Emilly Wheeler

Emily was a young woman with a gentle heart and a fierce spirit. She had long, curly brown hair and bright blue eyes that sparkled with intelligence and mischief. She was thin, with a lithe and athletic build, and her smile lit up her face and radiated warmth and kindness.

Emily was born and raised in Willow Creek, and had lived there her whole life. She was the youngest of three sisters, and had always felt a deep connection to her hometown. She was well-liked by everyone who knew her, known for her kindness, her wit, and her infectious laughter.

Emily was a free spirit, and loved to explore the world around her. She was fascinated by nature, and spent countless hours wandering through the forests and fields that surrounded her hometown. She loved to read, and had an insatiable thirst for knowledge, always eager to learn about new and interesting things.

But above all, Emily was driven by her love for Jack. From the moment she met him, she knew that he was the one, and she devoted herself entirely to their relationship. She was a fierce and loving partner, always there to support and encourage Jack, no matter what life threw their way.

Jack Williamson

And Jack was a young man of striking good looks, with chiseled features, sharp green eyes, and dark hair that was always styled perfectly. He was tall and broad-shouldered, with a muscular build that spoke of his athleticism and strength. Jack was confident and charismatic, and his easy smile and charming personality made him popular with everyone he met.

Growing up in Willow Creek, Jack had always been something of a local celebrity. He was a star athlete, excelling in both football and basketball, and his good looks and charm made him the envy of his classmates. But despite his success, Jack was a down-to-earth guy, with a warm and friendly personality that endeared him to those around him.

Jack was a natural leader, and his sense of responsibility and drive to succeed were qualities that made him stand out from the crowd. He had a big heart and a strong sense of morality, and he was always willing to help others, no matter what the cost. Jack was also a loyal friend, and his strong sense of loyalty and trustworthiness were qualities that those close to him held in high regard.

But despite all of his strengths, Jack had one weakness, and that was his love for Emily. From the moment he met her, he was smitten, and he devoted himself entirely to their relationship. He was a patient and loving partner, always there to support and encourage Emily, no matter what life threw their way.

2

The First Meeting...

———◦♡◦———

Having sensations of head over heels love is a typical encounter and can be areas of strength for a mind-boggling feeling. At the point when you meet somebody interestingly and have this inclination, it very well may be invigorating and nerve-wracking all simultaneously. It's normal to have sensations of apprehension and vulnerability, as you might be uncertain of how the other individual feels or acceptable behavior at the time.

Nonetheless, it's memorable's critical that head over heels love is in many cases simply an underlying fascination and may not be guaranteed to demonstrate a profound or dependable association. It's essential to take things slow, get to know the individual, and let the relationship grow normally.

Eventually, whether head over heels love prompts a fruitful and satisfying relationship relies upon many variables, including similarity, correspondence, and shared interests and values. In this way, it's OK to partake in the second and let the sentiments stream, however don't hesitate for even a moment to take as much time as necessary and get to realize the individual prior to going with any significant choices

So in this case, Emily had just lost her job at the local law firm and her apartment had been flooded, leaving her homeless and struggling to get back on her feet. She was feeling down on her luck and unsure of what the future held. On top of everything, it was pouring rain outside, making her day even worse. She took shelter from the rain in a small café, ordering a hot cup of coffee to warm her up.

As she sat there, trying to gather her thoughts, she couldn't help but feel like everyone around her was living their best life. The happy couple sitting across from her, laughing and holding hands, only made her feel worse. But just as she was about to lose all hope, she was greeted by a ray of sunshine in the form of a handsome young man named Jack. Full name Jack Williamson.

Emily in Cafe on a rainy day

"Hey there," Jack said, as he approached her table. "Do you mind if I sit here? All the other tables are taken."

Emily was taken aback by Jack's kindness. He was tall and broad-shouldered, with a charming smile that lit up his face. He had a kind energy about him that put her at ease, and before she knew it, they were chatting like old friends.

"So, what brings you here on such a rainy day?" Jack asked.

Emily hesitated for a moment, feeling embarrassed to admit her recent struggles. But as she looked into Jack's warm, inviting eyes, she found herself spilling her story. She told him about losing her job and her apartment, and how she was feeling lost and uncertain about the future.

Jack listened intently, offering her words of encouragement and support. He made her feel like everything was going to be alright, and for the first time in days, she felt a glimmer of hope.

As their conversation came to an end, Jack offered to walk her home, making sure she was safe in the rain. Emily was grateful for his help, and she couldn't help but feel like she had met someone special. As she said goodbye, she couldn't shake the feeling that this was just the beginning of something great.

Over the next few weeks, Emily and Jack continued to run into each other at the café, and their conversations grew longer and more meaningful. They talked about everything from their dreams and aspirations to their fears and insecurities. Emily was drawn to Jack's kind and caring nature, and she felt herself falling for him in a way she had never felt before. Sometimes at night they used to walk in a mist weather on a lonely road under yellowish street lights. At that place thier hands collapsed first.

"Oh! Sorry. It was my fault" Jack said. Emily said "No no not an issue" and she blushed quietly.

As their attraction grew, Emily couldn't help but feel like she was living a fairy tale. On her birthday, in the cold morning Jack was there out of his door with a heart shaped baloon and a red velvet cake. She had never imagined that she would find love in such unexpected circumstances, but here she was, falling head over heels for a man who seemed to be perfect in every way. But as early man said "No one is perfect".

But just as things seemed to be going perfectly, Emily and Jack would soon face their first challenge. A blast from Emily's past would threaten to tear them apart, and they would be forced to navigate a complicated web of emotions and past relationships. But through it all, Emily and Jack's love for each other would only grow stronger, proving that love truly can conquer all.

3

The Challenge...

Emily and Jack's relationship was going from strength to strength, and they were both head over heels in love with each other. However, as much as they wanted to believe that their love was all they needed to overcome any obstacle, they were soon faced with a challenge that threatened to tear them apart.

Emily received a phone call from her ex-boyfriend, David, who she hadn't heard from in years. He told her that he was in town and wanted to meet up with her to catch up. Emily was hesitant, knowing that her relationship with David had ended badly, but she agreed to meet with him out of curiosity.

Because 5 years ago,

One day, David met a girl named Emily in the office . She was kind, sweet, and innocent. David was attracted to her beauty, so he pretended to be in love with her and asked her out. Emily, who had never been in a relationship before, was over the moon and thought she had finally found true love.

As time went by, David's true colors started to show. He would constantly criticize and belittle Emily, making her feel small and worthless. But Emily loved David so much that she ignored all the red flags and stayed with him, hoping that one day he would change.

But that day never came. David became increasingly cruel, and Emily became more and more miserable. She tried to leave him multiple times, but every time she tried, David would apologize and promise to change, and Emily would always take him back.

One day, after yet another nasty argument, Emily finally mustered up the courage to end the relationship for good. She told Emily that she couldn't take his cruelty anymore and that she deserved to be treated with love and respect. David laughed in her face and told her that no one else would ever love her and that she should be grateful to have him.

But Emily was strong, and she walked away from Jack, never looking back. She learned to love herself and to never settle for less than she deserved. She found happiness and peace, and she never let anyone treat her badly again.

So now she want to know what is going on in his life. How guilt he is after leaving her or not?

When she told Jack about her plans to meet David, he was understandably upset. He didn't trust David and was worried about the impact he could have on their relationship. However, Emily was determined to be honest with Jack and make him understand that David was just a part of her past.

The meeting with David was more awkward than Emily had expected. He was still holding onto old feelings for her, and it was clear that he was trying to rekindle their relationship.David was begging crying, holding Emily's hand, promising her that this all will never happen again. David said he will kill Jack and he was very angry on Jack. After hearing this Emily slapped David and left that place.

Emily was caught in a difficult situation, not wanting to hurt David but also not wanting to give up her new relationship with Jack.

As she tried to navigate this complex situation, she realized that Jack was the one she truly loved and wanted to be with. She broke things off with David and returned to Jack, ready to work through their problems together.

However, Jack was still hurt and distrustful of David, and it took time for him to fully trust Emily and believe in their love again. The two of them spent long hours talking and working through their feelings,

"Are you upset?" Emily asked..

"No no", Jack replied with a fake smile on his face..

Emily holds Jack hand and said "I know you! You can't lie to me. You want to scold me or whatever you can do with me"

"Everything's solution is not to shout, beat or scold. I just want to know that why you were so curious to meet that David. Or still you have feelling for him. " Jack said..

Emily and Jack

After hearing this Emily hugged Jack in the middle of that lonely road under yellowish street and said "I can forget myself in your love, but I can never ever imagine of betraying you, Never!"

and in the end, their love proved to be stronger than any outside force.

Their relationship was put to the test, but in the end, Emily and Jack's love for each other triumphed. They had overcome the challenge and were now more committed than ever to each other. They had proven that love truly can conquer all, and that no matter what obstacles may come their way, they would always stand together for each other.

The rest of the summer was filled with laughter, love, and adventures as they explored their city and each other. They learned new things about each other every day and grew stronger in their love and commitment. Every Sunday they used to go to fishing. They knew that their relationship wasn't perfect, but they also knew that they were willing to put in the work to make it last. Relationship doesn't work only by caring, it can be carried easily by patience, respect towards each other, freedom, and lots of trust.

As the summer came to a close and Emily gets a new job in a new company, she felt like she was finally back on track. She was grateful for Jack and the love they shared, she knew that Jack was always there in her hard times and she knew that no matter what the future may bring, they would always have each other.

Emily and Jack's love story was far from over, and as they continued to navigate the ups and downs of life together, they learned that true love wasn't about never facing challenges, but about overcoming those challenges together. And as they looked forward to their future together, they knew that their love would only continue to grow stronger with each passing day.

Now Emily has started her work, sometimes she get late in the office. So, Jack felt possesive feeling towards Emily. According to me

Possessiveness in a love relationship refers to an excessive need to control or keep close tabs on one's partner, often driven by feelings of insecurity, jealousy, and a fear of losing the relationship. This can manifest in various ways, such as wanting to know your partner's every move, getting angry or upset if they talk to or spend time with other people, and trying to restrict their independence or freedom.

While a certain degree of possessiveness may seem natural in a romantic relationship, excessive possessiveness can be harmful and toxic. It can create an imbalance of power and control, leading to feelings of suffocation, restriction, and loss of personal autonomy. It can also lead to trust issues, conflicts, and even emotional and physical abuse.

To address possessiveness in a relationship, both partners need to work together to identify the root cause of the possessiveness and find ways to overcome it. This may involve open and honest communication, setting boundaries, building trust, and seeking help from a therapist or counselor if necessary. Ultimately, a healthy and happy relationship is built on mutual respect, trust, and a willingness to compromise and support each other's growth and well-being. But trust and believe can conquer everything which helps solve many such problems in Jack and Emily's life.

4
The Road Trip...

Emily and Jack had been together for a year now and their love was stronger than ever. They were excited to take a road trip together to celebrate their first anniversary and to make new memories that they could cherish forever. But Jack used to drink alcohol in absence of Emily as he was addicted but he didn't want that Emily feel bad because of this addiction.

The trip was going to be a surprise for Jack, and Emily had planned everything down to the last detail. She had researched the most scenic routes, the best places to eat, and the most romantic spots to visit.

Emily packed their bags, Jack quietly took a large bottle of alcohol with him and they set off early in the morning, eager to start their adventure. The first few hours of the drive were filled with laughter and music as they sang along to their favorite songs.

As they drove deeper into the countryside, the scenery around them became more and more breathtaking. It was quiet and far away from their daily chours noises with peace of mind.

They stopped at quaint little towns and tried local specialties, took walks by the river, and enjoyed the peace and quiet of the countryside. After crossing the river they saw dense forest, Emily couldn't resist she hold the hand of Jack and took him to the jungle for trek.

They were both nature lovers and were always looking for new and exciting adventures. So, when they saw that beautiful jungle in the heart of the countryside, they decided to go on a trip together.

The couple packed their bags and set out on the journey, excited for what was to come. They were amazed by the lush green vegetation and the sounds of the diverse wildlife as they hiked through the jungle.

As they were walking, they came across a beautiful waterfall surrounded by towering trees and colorful birds. Jack took out a picnic blanket and they sat down to enjoy a romantic lunch together. As they ate, they talked about their hopes and dreams, and the love they had for each other only grew stronger.

After lunch, they continued their trek and came across a group of monkeys swinging from tree to tree. Emily was in awe and couldn't resist taking photos to remember the moment. Jack took her hand and they stood there for a while, just watching the monkeys play.

They spent the night under the stars, surrounded by the beauty of the jungle. They felt grateful for the adventures they had shared and the love they had found in each other.

Their love for each other seemed to grow stronger with each passing mile, and they felt closer than ever before. They talked about their dreams and aspirations, and about the future they wanted to build together.

They reached their first destination, a beautiful cabin in the woods, just as the sun was setting. Emily had arranged for a candlelit dinner to be set up on the porch, and they sat and watched the stars twinkle above as they ate their meal and shared their thoughts and feelings with each other. Under moonlight, over a big rock they both were sitting Emily bend her head on Jack's shoulder . Jack holds Emily's hand and Emily was looking at the night's bright moon and sky and Jack was also looking at the sky, stars and moon but in her eyes. Then Emily suddenly looked at him and she asked "Any problem? My head is heavy?". He said "No no, It gives me relief I can do this all day". She kissed on his cheeks and blushed , and they slept. At midnight, Jack woke up took that bottle out from that bag and he goes near water and start drinking after 20 minutes he heard that Emily screams, he threw the bottle and ran towards the tent. He went inside the tent and tried to calm Emily. Jack grabbed her in his arms, she was crying, her heart was beating fast.

She asked "Where are you Jack? You are not with me from last few days. I want you, I can't lose you."

Jack smiled and said "I'm not going anywhere. How can a deadbody die?"

"Deadbody?" she asked

"Yes, at the age of 90s when you will die. Then I will die, first the soul has to leave the body. Mu soul is inside you." Jack said

"How cheesy and filmy!" Emily patted on his arms and said.

The next few days were a blur of adventure and romance. They visited wineries, went on hikes, and stargazed by a campfire. They talked about everything and anything, and their love for each other only grew stronger with each passing moment.

However, their road trip was not without its challenges. They had a flat tire in the middle of nowhere, they got lost on a hike, and they had a disagreement about which route to take. These challenges tested their patience and communication skills, but they always found their way back to each other and to the love that was at the core of their relationship.

As their road trip came to an end, they realized that the trip had brought them even closer together. They had shared new experiences and made memories that would last a lifetime. They had learned more about each other, and about themselves, and they had come to understand that their love was strong enough to overcome any challenge.

When they returned home, they felt like a new couple. They had a newfound appreciation for each other and a new understanding of what it means to be in love. They knew that their relationship was far from perfect, but they also knew that they were committed to making it work.

The road trip had taught them that love is not just about the big moments and grand gestures, but about the little things that make life worth living. They learned that true love is about being there for each other, through thick and thin, and about cherishing each other for who they are.

As Emily and Jack settled back into their daily routines, they felt a renewed sense of purpose in their relationship. They were grateful for the road trip, and for the love that they shared, and they knew that no matter what life may bring, they would always have each other.

And so, Emily and Jack continued on their journey together, with a love that only grew stronger with each passing day, and with a newfound appreciation for the power of love to conquer all obstacles. They knew that they had something special, and they were determined to make it last a lifetime.

5

The Next Stage...

Problems in life can bring a couple closer together by providing opportunities for them to work together and support each other. When faced with challenges, couples have the opportunity to strengthen their bond and deepen their connection as they navigate the difficulties together.

For example, overcoming a financial setback, supporting each other through a health crisis, or navigating a difficult life event such as the loss of a loved one can bring a couple closer as they rely on each other for emotional support and practical help. By working together and supporting each other, couples can build resilience and strengthen their relationship.

Additionally, facing problems can also provide an opportunity for couples to better understand each other's strengths and weaknesses, and to learn how to communicate more effectively. This can help to increase empathy, compassion, and mutual understanding within the relationship.

However, it's important to note that not all problems bring couples closer together. In some cases, problems can put a significant strain on a relationship and even lead to its downfall. The impact of problems on a relationship will depend on various factors such as the nature of the problem, the couple's individual coping styles, and the quality of their communication and support for each other.

It had been a year since Emily and Jack's road trip, so basically they were in relationship since 2 years and their love was stronger than ever. They had weathered many storms together and had grown closer with each passing day. They were confident in their relationship and knew that they were meant to be together forever.

When a boy is about to propose to the girl he loves, he is likely to experience a range of emotions. This can include feelings of excitement, nervousness, fear, and hope.

Excitement often stems from the anticipation of starting a new chapter in his life with the person he loves. He may be eager to express his love and commitment and to share his future with her.

Nervousness is a common emotion for many people when proposing. The boy may worry about how she will react and whether she will say yes. He may also feel pressure to make the moment perfect and memorable.

Fear can also be present as he worries about the possibility of rejection. This can cause him to second-guess his decision and wonder if he is ready for such a big step.

Finally, hope is also a common emotion. He may be filled with hope for a positive response and for a happy future together with the person he loves.

Overall, the feelings a boy experiences when proposing are likely to be a mix of emotions, but ultimately he is likely to be filled with love, excitement, and hope for the future.

On that day, Jack decided that it was time to take the next step in their relationship. He had been thinking about it for months, and he was finally ready to ask Emily to be his wife.

He planned a special evening, one that would be unforgettable for both of them. He took Emily to a rooftop restaurant, with a view of the city skyline, and set the stage for a proposal that would sweep Emily off her feet.

The restaurant was lit with candlelight, and soft music played in the background. A table was set for two, with a bouquet of roses and a bottle of champagne in the center.

As they sat down to dinner, Emily couldn't help but notice how nervous Jack seemed. She tried to make light of the situation, but Jack was too distracted to be his usual playful self.

Just as the main course was being served, Jack stood up and took a deep breath. He walked over to Emily, took her hand in his, and got down on one knee.

"Emily," he said, "I have loved you from the moment I met you. You are my best friend, my confidant, and my soulmate. I cannot imagine my life without you, and I want to spend the rest of my life making you happy. Will you do me the honor of becoming my wife?"

Emily was shocked and overwhelmed. She had always known that Jack was the one for her, but she never imagined that he would propose so soon. But she was afraid that her frienship will may get effected.

Tears welled up in her eyes as she looked at Jack, and she knew that there was only one answer she could give.

"Yes, Jack," she said, smiling through her tears. "I will be your wife."

They hugged and kissed each other, and Jack slipped a ring onto Emily's finger. It was a simple, yet elegant, diamond ring that sparkled in the candlelight.

The rest of the evening was a blur of excitement and joy. They called their families to share the news, and they toasted to their future together.

As the night came to an end, Emily and Jack walked hand in hand, back to their apartment. They talked about their future, about their plans for the wedding, and about the life they wanted to build together.

The next few months were a whirlwind of wedding preparations. Emily and Jack worked together to plan the perfect wedding, one that reflected their love and commitment to each other.

They picked a venue that was surrounded by nature, and they chose a color scheme that was inspired by the beauty of the countryside. They invited their families and friends, and they set a date that was special to both of them.

The day of the wedding arrived, and Emily was a bundle of nerves. She had always dreamed of her wedding day, but she never imagined that it would be this perfect.

She walked down the aisle, hand in hand with her father, and she saw Jack waiting for her at the end of the aisle. He was dressed in a black tuxedo, and his eyes were filled with love and happiness. When Jack saw her in wedding gown he was surprised, shocked, eyes filled with tears, and big smile in his face. His friends was there besides Jack they were patting his back, wooing in joy and happiness.

They exchanged vows, and as they said "I do," they knew that they were making a commitment to each other that would last a lifetime.

The reception was a night filled with laughter, love, and joy. Emily and Jack danced the night away, surrounded by their family.

6

Married Life...

Starting a new married life with a supportive husband can be an exciting time, but it can also come with its own set of challenges. Some of the difficulties that a girl may face include:

- Adjusting to a new home: Moving into a new home and setting up a shared life with your husband can take time and effort. You may need to make compromises and adjust to each other's habits and routines.
- Balancing work and family: If both partners are working, finding a balance between work and family life can be a challenge. It's important to communicate openly and find a solution that works for both of you.
- Maintaining independence: While it's important to support each other in a marriage, it's also important to maintain your own independence and individuality.
- Dealing with in-laws: In-laws can play a big role in a married couple's life, and it's important to find a way to build a healthy relationship with them.
- Managing finances: Money can be a sensitive topic in any relationship, and it's important to have open and

honest communication about finances and establish a budget that works for both partners.

Despite these challenges, a supportive husband can help make the transition into married life much smoother. It's important to communicate openly, be flexible, and work together to overcome any difficulties that may arise.

And by luck Emily has that support in the firm of Jack. Emily and Jack's honeymoon was a magical experience that they would never forget. They traveled to a remote island in the Pacific, where they spent two weeks relaxing and exploring the local culture. They returned home with a deeper appreciation for each other and with a newfound love for adventure.

However, once they returned to the real world, they soon realized that marriage was not always a bed of roses. They were now living together full-time, and they were discovering new challenges in their relationship.

Emily struggled to adjust to married life. She was used to having her own space and her own routine, but now she was sharing everything with Jack. She found it difficult to balance her work and her home life, and she was often exhausted by the end of the day.

Jack, on the other hand, was struggling with the new responsibilities of being a husband. He was used to coming and going as he pleased, but now he was responsible for supporting Emily and making their home a place of comfort and security.

They began to argue more often, and they found themselves struggling to communicate effectively. They were both feeling overwhelmed and frustrated, and they were starting to question their decision to get married.

They knew that they needed to find a way to work through their challenges, and they sought the help of a marriage counselor. The counselor taught them how to communicate effectively, how to listen to each other, and how to support each other through their challenges.

Over time, Emily and Jack learned how to work together as a team. They found a new appreciation for each other, and they discovered that marriage was not about living separate lives, but rather about living a shared life together.

Emily used to teach him yoga and helped him in cooking tutorials. While cooking it looks like Jack used to bath in that. And Jack used teach him fishing, martial arts and excercises and in the eyes of the world they proved themselves as the best couple.

They learned how to support each other, how to make each other feel loved and valued, and how to grow together as a couple. They found that the more they worked on their relationship, the stronger it became.

Their love for each other continued to grow, and they realized that they were meant to be together forever. They were each other's home, and they were each other's safe place.

Emily and Jack's marriage was far from perfect, but it was perfect for them. They had learned that love was not just about finding happiness, but it was also about working together to overcome challenges and to grow as individuals.

Their love was not just a feeling, but it was a choice that they made every day. They chose to love each other, to support each other, and to make each other a priority in their lives.

As they celebrated their first anniversary, Emily and Jack looked back on their journey and felt grateful for each other. They were stronger and more in love than ever, and they were looking forward to a lifetime of love and adventure together.

As they hugged each other, they knew that their love story was far from over, and that their journey together was just beginning. They had each other, and that was all that mattered. They were home.

7
Hard Times...

Emily and Jack's love story seemed to be going perfectly. They had overcome many challenges, and their love for each other had only grown stronger over time. But fate had other plans for them.

One early morning Emily woke up and do some yoga activities and then he went to make some tea, then after making tea she poured in kettle then she holds a tray and came in room opened the dooe of Jack's room put the tray on the center table, she lokked at him as while sleeping he looks cute, Emily get on bed hugged him and trying to wake him up, but she failed. She thought that he was doing prank on her. But half an hour passed, so Emily started panicing, her hands were shivering, eyes filled with tears, she called an ambulance. After reaching hospital doctor took him under observation then doctor said that , Jack was diagnosed with a rare and incurable illness. Emily was devastated. She had never thought that their love story would end like this. She had always imagined that they would grow old together, holding hands and smiling at each other like they had done on their wedding day.

But now, Jack was facing a difficult and uncertain future. He was struggling with the news of his illness, and he was starting to withdraw from Emily. He didn't want her to see him suffer, and he didn't want her to be burdened with his care.

Jack in hospital

Emily tried to be strong for Jack, but she was struggling with her own emotions. She was afraid of losing him, and she was afraid of what the future would bring. She felt like their love story was being taken away from them, and she didn't know how to make things right.

Despite Jack's illness, they continued to live their lives as best they could. They tried to stay positive and make the most of their time together. They went on trips and tried new things, hoping to create new memories that would sustain them through the difficult times ahead.

But as Jack's illness progressed, he became weaker and more dependent on Emily. He was in constant pain, and he was struggling to keep up with his daily routine. Emily was his primary caregiver, and she was struggling to balance her work and her home life.

She was exhausted, and she was starting to feel overwhelmed by the responsibilities of caring for Jack. She was trying her best to be strong for him, but she was also starting to feel hopeless about their future.

One day, Jack's condition worsened suddenly, and he was rushed to the hospital. Emily was beside herself with fear and worry. She didn't know what the future held, and she felt like she was losing the love of her life.

As she sat by Jack's bedside, she thought about all of the memories that they had created together. She thought about their first date, their wedding day, and their honeymoon. She thought about all of the moments of happiness that they had shared, and she realized that their love story was not just about their future, but also about their past.

When a person knows about a situation but feels powerless to change it, they may feel a range of emotions including frustration, anger, sadness, and helplessness. This feeling of being "stuck" or unable to act can be difficult to handle and can lead to feelings of hopelessness. In such situation they both supports each other. Emily used to cry in washroom by pressing her mouth, to keep silence. Jack knew everyhting, he can see her swollen eyes, her darkness under eyes that will soon entirely cover her life. Still while having meals he used to say

"Don't be upset dude. We will soon walk back home.". After hearing these things she wants to hold him in her arms for infinity.

Despite the tragedy of Jack's illness, Emily found comfort in the fact that they had shared a love that would last forever. She knew that even though Jack's time on this earth was coming to an end, their love story would live on in her heart forever.

As she held Jack's hand, she told him that she loved him and that she would always cherish the time that they had shared together. Jack smiled at her and said I will wait for you on another end and we will meet soon, she can't resist these words her tears rolled out and she walked out

Emily was heartbroken, but she also felt grateful for the time that they had shared together. She knew that Jack's death would be a devastating loss, but she also knew that their love story would live on in her heart forever. So, she ran away from the hospital because she was not able to see him in such condition.

As she said goodbye to Jack, she realized that the love story that they had shared was a rare and beautiful thing. It was a love that transcended time and that would last forever.

Despite the sadness and the tragedy of Jack's death, Emily was grateful for their love story. She knew that Jack would always be with her, and that their love story would continue to inspire others for generations to come.

Emily and Jack's love story may have come to a tragic end, but their love would live on forever.

8

Finding Peace...

It's difficult to describe the exact feelings of a person who has lost a loved one, as everyone experiences grief and loss differently. However, some common emotions that someone might feel after the death of a spouse include shock, disbelief, numbness, intense sadness, loneliness, anger, guilt, and depression. The process of grieving can be long and complex, and it often involves moving through a variety of different emotions as a person begins to come to terms with their loss. The individual may also feel overwhelmed by the practical considerations of life without their spouse, such as managing household responsibilities and finances. It's important to remember that everyone grieves at their own pace, and there is no right or wrong way to do so.

Emily was depressed

After Jack's death, Emily was left with a broken heart and a sense of emptiness. She felt like a part of her had been taken away, and she didn't know how to go on without him. She felt lost and alone, and she struggled to find meaning in her life.

In the days and weeks following Jack's death, Emily felt a deep sadness that she had never experienced before. She missed his presence in her life, and she felt like she was missing a part of herself. She tried to keep busy, but she found that nothing could fill the void left by Jack's absence.

Despite her grief, Emily found comfort in the memories that she had shared with Jack. She remembered their first date, their wedding day, and all of the other moments of happiness that they had shared together. She realized that their love story was a rare and beautiful thing, and she was grateful for the time that they had shared together.

As she struggled to come to terms with Jack's death, Emily realized that she needed to find a way to heal. She knew that she couldn't go on living with this sense of emptiness and sadness, and she realized that she needed to find a way to find peace.

Emily decided to take a trip, to get away from her daily routine and to try to find some clarity. She went to a remote location, where she could be alone with her thoughts and feelings.

During her time away, Emily reflected on her life and her relationship with Jack. She thought about all of the challenges that they had faced, and she realized that their love had been tested and proven to be strong. She realized that despite the tragedy of Jack's death, she was grateful for the love that they had shared.

As she spent time in nature, Emily found that she was able to connect with Jack in a way that she never had before. She felt his presence around her, and she felt like he was guiding her on her journey to find peace.

Emily realized that the love story that she and Jack had shared was not just about their past, but also about their future. She realized that their love would continue to inspire others for generations to come, and that their love story would live on forever.

Emily returned from her trip with a newfound sense of peace. She felt like she had come to terms with Jack's death, and she felt like she had found a way to honor his memory. She realized that their love story was not just about their time together on this earth, but about the love that would continue to live on in her heart.

Emily started to find joy in life again. She started to focus on the things that made her happy, and she started to look towards the future with hope and optimism. She realized that life was a journey, and that she had a bright future ahead of her.

She tried many things to cop up with this like:

1. Allow yourself to feel your emotions: It's important to allow yourself to feel and express your emotions, even if they are painful. Crying, talking to a friend, or writing in a journal can help you process your feelings.

2. Seek support: Talking to friends and family, or reaching out to a support group for people who have experienced similar losses, can provide comfort and help you feel less isolated.

3. Take care of yourself: Grief can be physically and emotionally draining, so it's important to take care of yourself. Eat well, exercise, and get enough sleep.

4. Find meaning: Consider volunteering, taking up a new hobby, or finding another way to give back and connect with others.

5. Remember your loved one: Create a memorial, share memories with others, or find other ways to keep your loved one's memory alive.

As she moved forward, Emily realized that Jack would always be with her, and that their love story would always be a part of her. She knew that she would never forget the love that they had shared, and that their love story would continue to inspire others for generations to come.

Emily and Jack's love story may have come to a tragic end, but their love would live on forever. Their love story was a testament to the power of love and the resilience of the human spirit. It was a love story that would inspire others for generations to come, and it was a love story that would never be forgotten.

9

Living Dead...

Five years had passed since Jack's death, and Emily was now an elderly woman. She had lived a fulfilling life, but she never forgot the love that she had shared with Jack.

Emily spent much of her time thinking about Jack and the memories that they had shared together. She remembered the way that he had made her laugh, the way that he had looked at her with love in his eyes, and the way that he had held her in his arms.

Emily also remembered the challenges that they had faced together. She remembered the way that they had supported each other through difficult times, and the way that their love had only grown stronger with each passing day.

Emily realized that the love that she and Jack had shared was a special and rare thing. She realized that their love story was not just about their time together on this earth, but about the love that would continue to live on in her heart.

Emily decided to honor Jack's memory by sharing their love story with others. She started to write about their love story, and she shared their story with anyone who would listen. She wanted to inspire others to find the love and happiness that she and Jack had shared.

Emily's love story touched the hearts of many people, and she received letters from people all over the world who had been inspired by her and Jack's love. She realized that her love story was not just her own, but it was a love story that belonged to everyone who had been touched by it.

Emily has been blessed with so much love in her life, and for that, she should be truly grateful. Love comes in many forms, from the love of family and friends to the love of a romantic partner. The love that Emily has received has likely shaped her into the person she is today and has provided her with the support and comfort she needs to face life's challenges.

The people who love Emily are a testament to her kind heart and warm personality. They appreciate her for who she is and are there for her through thick and thin. Their love is a constant source of strength and inspiration, and Emily should never forget how much they care for her.

It's important to take time to reflect on the love in one's life and to express gratitude for it. Emily should remind herself daily of the love that surrounds her and let those she loves know how much they mean to her. She should never take their love for granted, and should show her love in return by being there for them, just as they are always there for her.

Overall, the love Emily has received is a precious gift, and she should hold it close to her heart always.

Emily on her deadbed

As Emily approached the end of her life, she found peace in the knowledge that Jack's memory would live on through the love story that they had shared. She realized that their love story was a testament to the power of love, and that their love would continue to inspire others for generations to come.

On her deathbed, Emily closed her eyes for the final time, knowing that Jack was waiting for her on the other side. She was at peace, knowing that their love story would continue to live on in the hearts of others.

And so, Emily and Jack's love story came full circle. From the moment that they met, to the moment that they were reunited in death, their love story was a testament to the power of love and the resilience of the human spirit. It was a love story that would inspire others for generations to come, and it was a love story that would never be forgotten.

10

Flame Extinguished...

Emily's health had been declining for several months, and her family and friends could see that the end was near. They surrounded her with love and care, doing everything that they could to make her comfortable in her final days.

Despite her weakened state, Emily remained strong and determined. She wanted to spend her final moments surrounded by the people that she loved, and she wanted to share her love story one last time.

Emily summoned all of her strength to tell her family and friends about her and Jack's love story. She spoke with a smile on her face, and her eyes lit up as she relived the memories of her and Jack's life together.

Her family and friends listened with tears in their eyes, and they were filled with a sense of awe and inspiration. They realized that Emily's love story was a true testament to the power of love and the resilience of the human spirit.

As the days passed, Emily grew weaker and weaker, and her family and friends could see that the end was near. They gathered around her bedside, holding her hand and offering words of comfort.

Emily looked up at her loved ones and smiled, knowing that she was surrounded by love and peace. She closed her eyes for the final time, knowing that Jack was waiting for her on the other side.

And so, Emily passed away, surrounded by the love of her family and friends. Her love story had come to an end, but her legacy would live on in the hearts of those who had been touched by her and Jack's love.

Emily's death was a time of mourning and sadness, but it was also a time of celebration. Her family and friends celebrated her life and the love that she had shared with Jack. They knew that Emily was now reunited with the love of her life, and that she was at peace.

As they gathered to say their final goodbyes, Emily's family and friends realized that her love story was not just a story of two people in love, but a story of the power of love and the resilience of the human spirit. They realized that her love story was a testament to the fact that love can endure beyond death and that it can continue to inspire and touch the hearts of others for generations to come.

And so, Emily was laid to rest, surrounded by the love and memories that she had shared with Jack. Her love story had come full circle, from the moment that she and Jack had met, to the moment that they were reunited in death. It was a love story that would never be forgotten, and a love story that would continue to inspire and touch the hearts of others for generations to come.

11

The Heartbreak...

Life and love are magical and exceptional.

Life and love are two of the most important things that make our existence so meaningful and special. Love has the power to bring happiness, comfort, and joy into our lives, while life gives us opportunities for growth, learning, and making memories. When we are in love, life feels magical, and when we appreciate the magic of life, love becomes even more exceptional. Both life and love have their ups and downs, but ultimately, they are both gifts to be cherished.

Notice one thing that Emily didn't saw Jack's deadbody. As she told the hospital management to dispose Jack's body. And now see the miracle of life, due to that rare disease an unwanted protein started to generate in Jack's body which doctors recoverd later and Jack was not dead as presumed by Emily. So, doctors took him under her survillance and disconnected him from outer world. And jack also gets hope and he want to go back to Emily in a better condition. It tooks six years to recover that stage, he has gone under several blood treatments and medication just to see her wife again and to live a normal life. He was under super survillance as this could be dangerous or revolutionary in the field of science. But see how table turns, in hope of finding happiness. Actually Jack loses Emily. She ended her life in sorrow and finding happiness. And Jack started to recover he was happy with this as he will able to get back to his normal life with Emily.

The news of Emily's sudden death hit Jack like a ton of bricks. He couldn't believe that the love of his life was gone, and the thought of living without her was too much for him to bear. He was devastated, and the pain was so intense that he felt as though he was living in a nightmare from which he would never wake up.

For the first few days after Emily's death, Jack was in a state of shock. He wandered aimlessly through Willow Creek, unable to shake the sense of emptiness that had settled over him. He found it difficult to eat or sleep, and he felt as though he was slowly but surely losing his mind.

As the days turned into weeks, Jack began to realize that he needed to do something to cope with his grief. He started to spend more time outdoors, taking long walks through the woods, and immersing himself in nature. So, he went to that forest where they went on their roadtrip vacation in remembrence of Emily. He found that being surrounded by the beauty of the natural world helped to soothe his soul, and he felt a sense of peace that he had not experienced since Emily's passing.

Despite his efforts to heal, Jack still felt a deep sense of sadness and loss. He missed Emily more with each passing day, and the thought of living without her was too much for him to bear. He found that he could not shake the feeling that his life was meaningless and empty, and he struggled to find any sense of purpose or direction.

One day, Jack was out for a walk in the same woods when he stumbled upon a clearing he had never seen before. It was a peaceful, serene place, surrounded by tall trees, and he felt as though he had found a sanctuary from the world. As he stood there, taking in the beauty of the area, he heard a soft voice calling his name.

He turned to see a young woman standing before him, and he was struck by her beauty. She had long, curly hair, bright eyes, and a warm smile that lit up her face. Jack felt an instant connection to her, and he felt as though he had known her his entire life.

Restless Jack in Jungle

The woman introduced herself as Emily, and Jack was filled with a sense of joy and hope that he had not experienced in a long time. She explained to him that she had come to him as a spirit, and that she was there to help guide him through his grief and help him find a way to heal. As she has expirienced it earlier.

Over the next few weeks, Jack and Emily spent time together, talking and laughing and exploring the world around them. Jack found that his heart was starting to heal, and he felt a sense of joy and peace that he had not experienced since Emily's passing. He was grateful for her presence in his life, and he felt as though he had finally found a way to cope with his grief.

As their time together came to an end, Emily told Jack that she had to return to the afterlife, but that she would always be with him in spirit. Jack was filled with a sense of sadness as he watched her fade away, but he was also filled with a sense of peace, knowing that she was always there to guide and support him.

In the end, Jack learned that love never truly dies, and that even after death, it can still bring healing and comfort to those left behind. He found a way to cope with his grief, and he felt as though he had finally found a way to live again. And although he would never forget the love he had shared with Emily, he knew that their love would live on, forever and always.

After death also they support each other, they were connected, and this all we need to have a successful love life. But it exists in stories but rarely in reality.

The lesson from a tragic love story can vary, depending on the themes and events that unfold within the story. However, some lessons that can be derived from this story are:

- The fragility of love: A tragic love story often highlights the fact that love can be fragile and fleeting, even when two people are deeply in love. It shows that love is not enough to overcome all obstacles and that sometimes, despite one's best efforts, love can still fail.
- The importance of communication: Communication is a crucial part of any relationship, and a lack of communication can lead to misunderstandings and problems. In a tragic love story, the importance of communication is often emphasized and shown as a key factor in the failure of the relationship.
- The consequences of our actions: The characters in a love story often make choices that have a significant impact on their lives and the lives of those around them. A tragic love story highlights the importance of considering the consequences of our actions and how they can impact those we love.
- The value of true love: Despite its heartbreak, a tragic love story can still demonstrate the beauty and value of true love. It shows how two people can be deeply in love and that, even though their love may not last forever, it was still real and meaningful.
- The power of sacrifice: A love story can show the lengths to which someone will go for love, including making sacrifices for the person they love. In a tragic love story,

these sacrifices may not bring the desired outcome, but they demonstrate the depth of the love that the characters feel.

Not Every Story Ends Well...

A painful love story,
    That started with a smile,
    But there is no happiness in the end,
    There was only pain and loneliness.
    They became aware of each other,
    In the holy atmosphere of love,
    But some things in life's time,
    Started separating them.
    He has suffered the pain of love,
    But in the end he was alone,
    I can't find his smile anymore,
    Just a happy sad story.

What One Can Do!!...

Here are some general tips that can help improve one's love life:

1. Communication:

Communication is one of the most important aspects of a successful relationship. It involves the exchange of ideas, thoughts, and feelings between partners, and it's crucial for building trust, understanding, and intimacy.

Good communication requires active listening, empathy, and the ability to express oneself clearly. By sharing your thoughts and feelings with your partner, you can avoid misunderstandings and resolve conflicts effectively.

However, effective communication also involves being able to listen and understand your partner's perspective. This means setting aside your own opinions and biases, and trying to see things from their point of view.

Open and honest communication can also help partners understand each other's needs, expectations, and desires, leading to a deeper connection and greater satisfaction in the relationship.

In short, communication is the foundation of a healthy and successful relationship, and making an effort to communicate effectively can greatly improve the quality of your love life.

2. Emotional Intelligence:

The capacity to understand individuals on a deeper level alludes to an individual's capacity to comprehend and deal with their own feelings, as well as the feelings of others. In a relationship, the capacity to understand people at their core can assist accomplices with seeing each other's feelings and answer in manners that are strong and cherishing.

Individuals with high capacity to understand people on a deeper level will generally be more mindful, and they have a superior comprehension of what their activities and words mean for other people. This can prompt better correspondence and compromise, as well as a more grounded connection between accomplices.

Having the capacity to appreciate people on a deeper level likewise implies having the option to control one's own feelings, which can be especially useful in troublesome or unpleasant circumstances. By dealing with their own feelings, accomplices can stay away from automatic responses that can raise clashes and on second thought answer in a more smart and useful manner.

The capacity to understand people on a deeper level is an expertise that can be created over the long haul through self-reflection, mindfulness, and a readiness to learn and develop. By rehearsing the capacity to understand people on a profound level in your relationship, you can construct a more profound association with your accomplice and work on the general nature of your adoration life.

3. Trust:

Trust is a foundation of any fruitful relationship. It includes believing in your accomplice's trustworthiness, uprightness, and unwavering quality, and it's fundamental for building major areas of strength for a steady association.

At the point when trust is available seeing someone, can be more open and open to one another, knowing that their sentiments, considerations, and activities will be regarded and esteemed. Trust likewise prompts more prominent closeness and a feeling that all is well with the world, as accomplices feel sure that their relationship depends on shared regard and backing.

Building trust in a relationship requires consistency, genuineness, and straightforwardness. It implies staying true to your commitments and being transparent about your viewpoints, sentiments, and activities. It additionally includes assuming the best about your accomplice and staying away from ways of behaving that could subvert trust, like lying, cheating, or being mysterious.

On the off chance that trust is broken seeing someone, can be hard to fix, yet at the same it's certainly feasible. To revamp trust, accomplices should be straightforward, apologize, and cooperate to remake a groundwork of common regard and understanding.

4. Quality Time:

Hanging out is a significant method for reinforcing the connection among accomplices and work on the general nature of a relationship. Quality time permits accomplices to associate, share encounters, and fabricate recollections together.

Quality time can incorporate exercises like date evenings, excursions, and side interests that you both appreciate. It means quite a bit to try to get to know each other consistently, and to focus on it in any event, when life gets going.

Hanging out can likewise assist accomplices with remaining associated and in total agreement, in any event, when they're not genuinely together. It permits accomplices to stay aware of one another's lives, and to remain in a state of harmony sincerely and intellectually.

Quality time can take many structures, yet mainly, it's time spent together that is significant, deliberate, and zeroed in on building your relationship. Whether you're attempting another eatery, going for a stroll, or simply nestling on the sofa, the objective is to make extraordinary minutes and encounters that reinforce your bond.

5. Adaptability:

Connections are continually developing and changing, and an effective love life expects accomplices to be adaptable and versatile. This implies being available to change, able to attempt new things, and ready to conform to new conditions as they emerge.

Having an adaptable and versatile way to deal with connections can assist accomplices with conquering difficulties and explore life's highs and lows together. It permits them to track down clever fixes to issues, and to adjust to one another's changing necessities and wants.

Being adaptable and versatile likewise implies being willing to think twice about to see things according to your accomplice's point of view. This can assist accomplices with settling on some mutual interest, and it can keep clashes from raising and harming the relationship.

It's memorable's essential that connections are dynamic and continually changing, and being open and versatile can assist accomplices with building major areas of strength for a strong relationship that can endure any hardship.

6. Emotional Support:

Consistent reassurance is pivotal for a fruitful love life. It includes being there for one another, giving solace and grasping in the midst of hardship, and aiding each other develop and create.

Having an accomplice who offers close to home help can assist people with feeling esteemed, appreciated, and comprehended. It can likewise build convictions that all is good and security in a relationship, as accomplices realize they have somebody to go to when they need it.

To offer profound help, accomplices should be great audience members, and to be receptive to one another's requirements and concerns. It's likewise essential to show sympathy and understanding, and to be non-critical and strong in troublesome times.

As well as offering profound help, looking for help from your partner is additionally significant. This implies being transparent about your necessities, and requesting help and backing when you want it.